MARVEL HEROES

MOVIE THEATER STORYBOOK

Adapted by Michael Teitelbaum

CONTENTS

Reader's Digest Children's Books

New York, New York • Montréal, Québec • Bath, United Kingdom

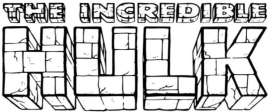

THE INCREDIBLE HULK

Dr. Bruce Banner was a brilliant scientist. Banner worked at the U.S. Defense Department's nuclear research facility at Desert Base, New Mexico. There, he worked on a project that was attempting to harness the awesome power of gamma radiation. Banner created a new weapon based on gamma radiation, called the G-bomb.

A test explosion of the new weapon was set up in an empty expanse of desert near the research facility. "If the G-bomb works as planned, it will become the most powerful weapon on Earth," Banner told his fellow scientists.

DISK 1

1

One of those scientists, a man named Igor Starsky, was actually a foreign spy. He hoped to steal the secrets of the G-bomb. But Banner kept the secrets to himself.

"Why won't you share the secret of your gamma bomb with the rest of us?" Starsky asked angrily.

Before Banner could respond, General "Thunderbolt" Ross, the man in charge of the G-bomb project, burst into the base's control room. "What's the delay, Banner?" Ross asked gruffly. "Are you going to test that bomb or not?"

Banner pressed a button on the control panel. "I've started the final countdown, General," he announced. "The bomb should go off in less than one minute."

Then Banner grabbed a pair of binoculars and peered out the window to watch the explosion. "Wait!" he cried suddenly. "There's someone driving into the test area!"

Banner raced toward the door. "Igor, stop the countdown!" he shouted. "I'm going to get that boy out of there!"

"Sure," Igor replied. But he had no intention of stopping the countdown. If Banner won't share his secrets, then he will perish in the explosion, Igor thought.

Meanwhile, Banner quickly reached the car on the test site. It was driven by a teenage boy. "What are you doing here?" Banner shouted. "You have to get out of here now!"

"My friends dared me to sneak out here," the boy explained.

 "You fool!" Banner cried, pulling the boy from his car and shoving him into a protective trench. But before Banner could jump into the trench himself, the bomb went off. **KABOOM!**

Bruce Banner was struck by the full force of the explosion. Waves of gamma radiation washed over his body. When he woke up  hours later, Banner discovered that he was at home. The teenager that Banner had saved stood beside him.

"How did I get here?" Banner asked the teenager, his head throbbing.

"I brought you," said the teenager. "It was the least I could do since you saved my life. I'm Rick Jones."

"Why didn't Igor stop the countdown?" Banner asked, growing angry.

As Banner grew more and more enraged, his heart started beating faster. His pulse quickened and he began sweating. Then Rick Jones looked on in amazement as Bruce Banner underwent an astonishing transformation.

His body grew to three times its normal size. His skin turned bright green. Bursting out of his clothes, Banner had disappeared completely. In his place stood the huge monster known as the Incredible Hulk!

When Banner's body changed, his mind did, too. He was no longer the brilliant scientist. Instead, he had become a raging beast. The Hulk smashed right through the wall of his house and stormed out into the countryside. General Ross sent a squad of soldiers to stop him.

"Leave me alone!" Hulk shouted, slamming into an army jeep with his massive fists. He crushed the car as if it were made of paper. Then he lifted the jeep over his head and

11 ▶ tossed it away like a toy.

"Fire!" shouted the sergeant. His troops opened fire with a barrage of bullets and grenades. They all bounced harmlessly off the

12 ▶ Hulk's thick green skin.

The Hulk punched a nearby mountain,

13 ▶ shattering it into boulders. Then he grabbed a huge boulder and flung it at the soldiers.

"Retreat! Retreat!" shouted the sergeant. "We can't stop that enormous monster!"

The Hulk leaped into the air. He kept rising higher and higher. When he landed several miles away in a single bound, he

14 ▶ opened up a huge crater in the earth.

Finally free from his attackers, the Hulk sat quietly. Slowly, he changed back into Bruce Banner.

"Why did this happen to me?" Banner cried out. "How can I go on living, knowing there is a monster inside me?"

And so, Bruce Banner's nightmare began. Each time he got angry, he would once again turn into the Incredible Hulk!

Not really a hero or a villain, the Hulk remained a mystery to both those who fear him and those who try to be his friend. As one of the strongest super-beings in the world, the Hulk joined the Super Hero team known as The Avengers. But even his partners in that group—Iron Man, Thor, Ant-Man, and the Wasp—could never figure out the Green-Skinned Goliath, so he left. He later joined The Defenders, teaming up with Dr. Strange and the Sub-Mariner, but only when his presence was required.

Through it all, though, the Hulk remains a well-meaning, lonely, and misunderstood figure.

15

16

AVENGERS

In Asgard, the realm of the Gods, Loki, the God of Evil, hatched a plan to free himself. "My brother Thor, the God of Thunder, trapped me here in Asgard," Loki said. "I must lure him here and defeat him. Only then shall I be free."

Loki used his power of mental projection to send an image into the mind of the Incredible

DISK 1

1

Hulk back on Earth. The Hulk believed he saw dynamite on a train track, but the dynamite wasn't really there.

"I must save that train!" said the Hulk, as he landed with enormous force on the tracks. The tracks shattered, just as a train came barreling toward the Hulk.

The Hulk used his incredible strength to hold up the tracks as the train passed safely by. But then the Hulk was accused of attacking the train, and the Emerald Behemoth was once again on the run.

2▶ "I can't believe the Hulk did this," said Rick Jones, the Hulk's best friend. Jones sent out an urgent radio message asking for the Fantastic Four to help find his friend. But Loki used his magic to divert the signal to the Mighty Thor.

"Why did you send for me?" Thor asked when he arrived at Jones's home.

Before Jones could answer, three other Super Heroes also arrived—Iron Man, and the tiny heroes, Ant-Man and the Wasp.

"Seems we all got your signal," Iron Man said to Jones. Then the heroes set out to find the Hulk.

Thor spotted him first. "My mighty hammer will stop him!" Thor cried.

Thor flung his enchanted hammer, but it passed right through the Hulk. Then the Hulk faded from sight.

"This isn't really the Hulk!" Thor exclaimed. "It's a mental image.

Only my evil brother, Loki, is capable of such wizardry. I must journey to Asgard at once!"

5
And so, while the Mighty Thor traveled across the Rainbow Bridge to the mystic realm of Asgard, the others continued their search for the Hulk.

"There he is!" shouted the Wasp, as the
6
Green-Skinned Goliath bounded across the mountainous countryside.

Iron Man grabbed the Hulk, but the Emerald Behemoth slammed him with a mighty fist. Iron Man crashed to the ground.

"Wait!" Iron Man shouted, as the Hulk bounded away. "I want to help you. You can trust me!"

"Bah!" the Green-Skinned Goliath grumbled. "I don't trust anybody!"

Meanwhile, in Asgard, Thor battled his evil brother, Loki. "My hammer will punish you, Loki!" Thor said, flinging the mighty mallet.

But Loki used his magic to create an icy shield that blocked the hammer.

Thor grabbed his enchanted hammer and swung it again. This time it shattered the ice shield. "Nothing can save you now, prince of evil!" Thor bellowed.

But Loki summoned the Trolls—the natural enemies of the Gods of Asgard. The huge beasts burst from the ground and grabbed Thor.

"No one can escape the grip of a Troll!" Loki cackled evilly.

But the God of Thunder had a plan. He pounded his enchanted mallet on the ground, summoning a blaze of lightning. The Trolls shrieked in pain and released Thor.

"The eyes of these underground creatures cannot bear the brightness of my lightning!" Thor shouted. "And now, Loki, you are coming with me!" Thor unleashed the enchanted power of his hammer, which pulled Loki to it like a powerful magnet.

When Thor returned to Earth with Loki, he found Iron Man, Ant-Man, and the Wasp battling the Hulk.

11

"Stop!" Thor shouted. "You have no reason to fight. The Hulk is innocent. Loki planned the train wreck to draw me to him."

12

Thor then banished Loki back to imprisonment in Asgard.

"We should work as a team," Iron Man suggested.

"Each of us has different powers," the Wasp said.

"If we combine our powers we could be unbeatable!" Ant-Man added.

"I am tired of being chased," the Hulk said. "Like it or not, I'm joining you."

"We will never be beaten," Thor announced, raising his mighty thammer. "For we are The Avengers!"

Weeks later, while patrolling under the ocean in their submarine, The Avengers spotted a human figure encased in a block of ice.

Bringing the frozen figure onboard, The Avengers chipped away the ice and made a startling discovery. "This is the great war hero, Captain America!" the Wasp cried. "I recognize his costume. But he disappeared many, many years ago!"

13 ▶ Suddenly, Captain America awakened. Thinking he was surrounded by enemies, he attacked The Avengers.

14 ▶ "You cannot defeat me!" Captain America shouted, dodging Thor's mighty hammer.

"Are you the real Captain America?" Iron Man asked, diving at the costumed figure.

Captain America dropped to the floor and kicked out with his feet in one smooth motion, sending Iron Man flying.

"He's for real, all right," said Iron Man. "But how could it really be you?"

15

"I was frozen in that ice for all these years," Captain America explained. "It must have kept me alive. But now I have returned."

The others invited Captain America to join The Avengers. In time, the great warrior became their leader. When trouble struck, Captain America raised his mighty shield and cried: "Avengers assemble!"

With those words, the powerful Super Hero team swung into action. And from then on, whenever and wherever evil was to be found, The Avengers were there to take a heroic stand against it.

16